First published 2002 by Walker Books Ltd
87 Vauxhall Walk, London SE11 5HJ

2 4 6 8 10 9 7 5 3 1

Text © 2002 Anne Fine
Illustrations © 2002 Penny Dale

The right of Anne Fine to be identified as
author of this work has been asserted by her in accordance
with the Copyright, Designs and Patents Act 1988

This book has been typeset in Giovanni Book

Printed and bound in Great Britain
by Creative Print and Design (Wales), Ebbw Vale

British Library Cataloguing in Publication Data:
a catalogue record for this book
is available from the British Library

ISBN 0-7445-5965-0

The Jamie & Angus Stories

Anne Fine

Illustrated by Penny Dale

WALKER BOOKS
AND SUBSIDIARIES
LONDON · BOSTON · SYDNEY

Other books by Anne Fine include:

Contents

Dry-Clean Only

Jamie saw Angus staring forlornly
out of the shop window. His silky coat
looked smooth as bathwater
and white as snow.

"Oh, please," begged Jamie. "Please can I have him for my birthday?"

"Your birthday was last week," Mummy said, trying to tug him past.

But Jamie wouldn't budge. "Christmas, then?"

"Christmas is not for *months*," his mother said. "By then you'll probably want something else."

"No, I won't," Jamie insisted. He pressed his nose up hard against the glass and gazed at Angus. Angus gazed at him.

"Oh, please," said Jamie. *"Please."*

"All right," said Jamie's mother. "I'll get him. But that's what you're having for Christmas even if you change your mind. And you're not having him even one day early."

"I'll wait," said Jamie. "I promise I won't grumble. I'll just wait."

Angus spent all the autumn and half the winter stuck in a plastic bag. His head was allowed to poke out so that he could breathe. He was put so high up in the cupboard that Jamie couldn't reach him. He could only wave.

But Jamie kept busy. First he made a farm for Angus
to live on. He patched fields together
from all the green and brown
scraps in the sewing basket,

painted lavatory-roll tubes
to look like hedges,

and built several splendid
five-barred gates out of
lollipop sticks.

He made a fir tree out
of Granny's old loofah,

and a pond out of the mirror
from one of her face
powder compacts.

And every day he kept Angus up to date on how long they still had to wait before they could be together properly.

When he'd finished the farm, Jamie built Angus a cattle shed out of shoeboxes and corrugated paper. It was a bit messy, but it was the right size, had a good view of the pond and looked very comfortable.

"I think you'll be happy in it," Jamie told Angus. "Cosy and safe on dark nights, and in storms."

Angus gazed down admiringly.

At last all the days passed. On Christmas Eve Angus disappeared from the top of the cupboard, and under the tree appeared a funny-shaped package with legs and horns, and two tiny holes punched in the snouty bit so it could breathe.

"See you tomorrow," Jamie whispered to the package.

The package rustled its paper excitedly.

On Christmas morning Jamie opened his present and he and Angus were together properly for the first time. Angus adored his spacious greeny-brown fields. He felt proud and confident behind his fine painted hedges. He admired his pond. And he was very, very happy in his shed. Jamie was in seventh heaven. He'd waited so long to bury his face in that magnificent silky coat, as smooth as bathwater and white as snow.

The only thing he wasn't sure about was the horrid tickly label behind Angus's ear that said DRY-CLEAN ONLY.

"What does it mean?" he asked his mother.

"It means he can't go in the washing-machine," his mother explained. "If he gets grubby, he'll have to go to Speediclean with all my suits and fancy dresses."

Jamie knew Angus had heard. Next time they went to Speediclean, he felt him tremble in his arms. The glue smell was terrible, and the giant machines juddered and roared.

Jamie leaned closer, till the horrid label tickled his cheek. "Don't worry," he whispered in Angus's gorgeous silky white ear. "I promise you'll never, *ever* have to come here. I'll keep you clean."

Angus gazed up at him trustingly.

So, because they would

never need it (and it was horrid and tickly), next time he was mending one of Angus's fields, Jamie used the sewing scissors to cut off Angus's little DRY-CLEAN ONLY label and threw it in the bin.

"There," he warned Angus sternly. "Now stay clean."

But Angus couldn't. He charged over his fields so fast, he kept crashing through his hedge and sliding under the bookcase into the dust and the cobwebs. Once, when his shed was being mended, he got mixed up with all the muddy boots. And when Jamie was touching up the lolly-stick gates, he got sticky with glue and tipped over a paint pot.

"He's looking pretty scruffy," Mummy observed.

"Downright insanitary," said Granny.

Jamie just held Angus tighter. But one day, while Jamie was away at nursery school, Granny picked up poor Angus, frowned at the mess of dust and mud and glue and cobwebs and paint, and put him in the washing-machine with the towels and the flannels.

She poured in the powder and pressed the on button.

Disaster! When Angus came out, his silky white coat was gone, and in its place was a shaggy grey tangle. He didn't look like Angus at all.

He looked terrible. *Terrible!*

When Jamie came home and saw him, he burst into tears.

"Never mind." Mummy tried to comfort him. "Perhaps he'll look better when he's a bit drier."

But he didn't. If anything, he looked even worse.

"He should have had a label," Granny said. "He should have said DRY-CLEAN ONLY. Then it would never have happened."

Jamie said nothing. He just cried even harder. Angus spent that night in the kitchen. And the next.

(Mummy said he was still too damp to be anywhere else.) But on the third morning, at breakfast time, Jamie found a funny-shaped package next to his plate.

From Granny, said the label. DRY-CLEAN ONLY.

Jamie took off the wrappings while Angus watched anxiously.

"I hope you like him," said Granny. "He's exactly the same."

He was, too. His silky coat was smooth as bathwater and white as snow. Jamie buried his face in it. It felt *perfect* (except for the tickly label).

Jamie took a good long look at Angus, still waiting patiently near the heater, all damp and grey and

bedraggled. Then he looked at the present from Granny, all proud and silky and shining and new.

Maybe he'd be too proud to charge round the greeny-brown patch fields like Angus. Maybe he wouldn't think much of a shed made out of a shoebox. Maybe he'd laugh at the painted cardboard-tube hedges and the lollipop-stick gates. Maybe he'd think the mirror pond wasn't big enough.

Maybe he wouldn't be as happy as Angus. Or as much of a friend.

Jamie handed the lovely new present back to Granny. "I think he should go back to the shop," he said firmly. "So he can find someone else."

Granny looked puzzled. "I thought you wanted one with a silky white coat."

"Yes," Jamie said. "I thought I did too. But now I know that all I want is Angus."

Angus and Jamie still play together almost every day. Angus still loves his farm. But now he's scruffy and grubby-looking, he can go anywhere without worrying. And when he gets absolutely disgusting, Granny puts him back in the washing-machine with the towels and the flannels and his greeny-brown fields.

He stares hopefully out of the little glass window, while Jamie fixes the cattle shed with sticky tape and repaints the hedges.

Both of them waiting till they can be together again. Angus and Jamie. Jamie and Angus.

Uncle Edward Teaches Angus to Jump

Bedtime. But Jamie really didn't
want to go upstairs.

Uncle Edward had come for a visit and Jamie didn't see why he should have to miss all the chatter and fun just because of stupid old bedtime.

"I'm not tired," he kept telling everyone.

"Maybe you're not," said his father. "But it's still bedtime, so you have to go."

"I'll take you up," said Uncle Edward. "I've never put anyone to bed before. It'll be good to start with someone like you, who knows what he's doing."

Jamie's mother laughed. "I hope you make a better job of putting Jamie to bed than you do with yourself." (Uncle Edward was famous for staying up late and not wanting to get up in the morning.)

So Jamie kissed Mummy and Daddy and took Uncle Edward's hand. "You have to say 'Up the little wooden hill to Dreamland' now," he told him.

"Do I?" said Uncle Edward.

"Yes," Jamie said.

So Uncle Edward said, "Up the little wooden hill to Dreamland," and they went up the stairs.

When they reached Jamie's room, Uncle Edward sat down on the carpet in the doorway.

"Right," he said cheerfully. "Go on, then. Get on with it."

"I thought you were supposed to be putting me to bed," said Jamie.

"No," Uncle Edward said. "You're putting yourself to bed. Angus and I are just watching." He swivelled round and put his feet halfway up one side of the doorway and balanced Angus on his stomach.

Jamie folded up his clothes and found his pyjamas, and climbed over Uncle Edward and Angus to get out onto the landing to put his socks and pants in the laundry basket. Then he climbed back over them both to draw his curtains and put on his reading lamp and turn his clock to face the exact right way. Then he climbed back over Uncle Edward and Angus to go to the bathroom and clean his teeth and fill his bedside beaker with fresh water.

"Aren't you coming to check that I clean my teeth properly?" he asked Uncle Edward.

"No," Uncle Edward said. "We'll soon know if you

don't, because they'll go black and fall out much sooner than expected."

Jamie cleaned his teeth even more properly than usual.

When he came back, Uncle Edward and Angus were lying on the bed. "This is a whole lot more comfy than that doorway," Uncle Edward said. "What now?"

"You read me a story," explained Jamie.

Uncle Edward sat up on the bed. "I know," he said. "We'll toss for it. Heads, I read you a story. Tails, you read one to me."

"No," Jamie insisted. "You have to read the story."

So Uncle Edward read the story. Then he switched off the lamp. "I'm off back downstairs now," he said to Jamie. "Happy?"

"No," Jamie said, because really he wanted to be downstairs with everybody in the chatter and the light, not stuck up in his nearly dark bedroom with Angus, the two of them all by themselves. "Can't you stay just till I go to sleep?"

"I'll half stay," offered Uncle Edward. "I'll stay in the doorway with Angus. Then I'll be half back with them and half here with you."

"All right," said Jamie, "but you must promise to remember to put Angus safely in his shoebox shed before you leave, because that's where he sleeps."

"I won't forget," said Uncle Edward.

So Jamie shut his eyes and tried to go to sleep. After a while Uncle Edward started whistling softly.

Jamie opened his eyes. "I can't sleep if you're whistling," he scolded.

So Uncle Edward stopped whistling. Jamie shut his eyes and tried to sleep again. It was quiet for a bit, then Uncle Edward started running one of Jamie's little plastic tractors over the tiny ribs in the carpet. "*Vroom-vroom. Vroom-vroom.*"

Jamie opened his eyes. "I can't go to sleep if you keep going *vroom-vroom*," he explained.

Uncle Edward sighed. "I can't whistle and I can't go *vroom-vroom*," he said. "So what am I supposed to sit here doing?"

But Jamie didn't know, because when Mummy and Daddy and Flora the babysitter put him to bed, all they did was read him a story and then leave the door ajar so he could see a slice of warm light from the landing. None of them ever lay on their back in the doorway with their head up one side of the door and their feet up the other, and Angus standing on their stomach.

"I'm not sure," he said. "Maybe you're just supposed to lie there quietly, doing nothing."

"That's a bit dull," said Uncle Edward. "I'll tell you what. I'll spend the time usefully, teaching Angus how to jump."

Jamie sat up in bed. "Angus can't—"

"Sssh!" Uncle Edward interrupted him. "Lie down and shut your eyes. And don't say a word because Angus has to concentrate."

So Jamie lay down and pretended to shut his eyes while Uncle Edward took Angus off his stomach and stood him on the carpet. "Right, Angus," he told him. "We'll start with something really simple." He glanced at Jamie. "You're not peeping, are you?"

"No," Jamie lied.

"Yes, you are," Uncle Edward said. "I can tell. But you mustn't. It isn't fair on Angus. Not while he's learning."

And Uncle Edward sailed Angus over his stomach and put him down on the carpet on the other side, where Jamie couldn't see him.

"Right," he said. "We'll begin with a little hop and a skip, just to warm up."

In the dark, Jamie heard a tiny thudding noise, as if Angus were hopping and skipping on the carpet.

"That's good," said Uncle Edward. "Well done, Angus. That's a very fine start."

Jamie sat up. "But Angus doesn't—"

"Sssh!" Uncle Edward interrupted him. "You mustn't distract Angus while he's having his lesson."

So Jamie lay down and shut his eyes again.

"Right, Angus," said Uncle Edward. "Now we'll do a backwards somersault, all the way over and round. It's a little bit fancy, but I think that you'll manage it."

There was another soft thudding noise, as if Angus were doing a backwards somersault, all the way over and round.

"Excellent!" said Uncle Edward. "You're a born jumper, Angus."

Jamie sat up again, but he couldn't see anything because Uncle Edward was in the doorway. So he lay down and shut his eyes again.

"Now, Angus," said Uncle Edward. "We'll try your first head over heels roly-poly. But remember to tuck your hooves in, or you'll get all untidy and trip over them. Ready?"

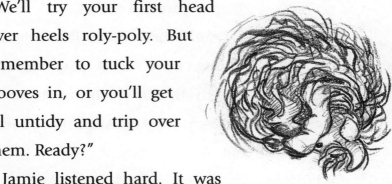

Jamie listened hard. It was easier with his eyes closed. First he heard a few soft thuds along the carpet, as if Angus were cantering to get up speed. Then there was a little silent wait, as if Angus were flying head over hooves in the air. And then there was a big thud.

"Brilliant!" said Uncle Edward. "That was really good."

33

Jamie sat up again. "Can I watch?"

"No. Not while he's practising. Wait till he's perfect."

So Jamie lay back and listened. Deep in the dark, with his eyes tightly closed, it was easy to see all the things he was hearing. When Uncle Edward said, "Right, Angus. Now we're going to jump off all four hooves at

once, up really, really high," he could almost see Angus shooting up as fast as a rocket.

And when Uncle Edward said, "Now, how about a great fancy twirl in the air?" in his head he could clearly see Angus spinning round so fast that his hooves

nearly got tangled.

On and on went the lesson, with Uncle Edward's voice getting softer and softer, and the jumps getting fancier and fancier, and Angus getting more and more perfect, till Jamie heard Uncle Edward whispering, "And now, Angus, we're going to do an amazing, astonishing, wonderful double fancy backwards bounce with treble spin and extra twirl; and after that I want you to just keep rising up as high and high as you can go – up, up and up…"

And, with his eyes still tightly closed, Jamie saw Angus do one last amazing, astonishing, wonderful double fancy backwards bounce with treble spin and extra twirl, and then rise up as smoothly and calmly and perfectly as a let-go balloon, up, up and up, almost as high as the ceiling, then out of the

open window on the landing
and up some more, into the shadowy blue
moonlit sky, up, up and up, on and on, higher and
higher, till he was floating over silvered clouds,
floating and floating and floating
and floating…

In the morning, when Jamie woke up, he saw Angus standing safely in his shed, not looking any different from usual, except that on his hooves were tiny specks of fluff, the same colour as the carpet on the landing.

Jamie carried him through to where Uncle Edward was sleeping and plonked him on the bed.

"Go on," challenged Jamie. "Show me. Now that he's finished practising, show me how Angus can jump."

Uncle Edward opened one eye and groaned. "Go on, then," he told Angus. "Now that you're perfect, show him. Jump."

Angus just stood there with carpet fluff on his hooves.

"See?" Jamie said. "Angus can't—"

"Sssh!" Uncle Edward interrupted. "You mustn't say anything to upset him. It's just that he's forgotten. You know what this means, don't you? It means I'll have to put you to bed again tonight, to give him another lesson."

And, thinking he'd enjoy that more than arguing, Jamie left poor tired Uncle Edward to sleep and went down to have breakfast with Mummy and Daddy.

Flora's
Wedding

Flora the babysitter

was going to get married.

She had a white dress with pretend pearls embroidered all over it. She had the prettiest satin slippers. And she had two daisy hairslides to hold back her tumbling hair.

And she wanted to have her wedding party in a field full of buttercups.

"Suppose it rains," said Jamie's mother.

"It won't rain," said Flora.

"Won't it be difficult to get the wedding cake safely into the field?" asked Jamie's father.

"No," Flora told him. "Even fields have gates."

"Angus will like it," said Jamie. "Angus loves fields. And he'll especially like a field full of buttercups."

So as soon as Jamie's mother and father had kissed Jamie goodbye and gone out, Flora and Jamie sat down and made Angus his very own invitation:

After the Wedding,
Come to the Buttercup Field
with everyone
for a Grand Party
(with special fly-away wishing balloons)

"What's a special fly-away wishing balloon?" asked Jamie.

"It's a balloon with a special wish written on it," said Flora.

"And does it really fly away?" asked Jamie.

"Oh, yes," said Flora.

"How high?" asked Jamie.

"Wait and see," said Flora.

So Jamie waited. He waited while Flora and her boyfriend Mark stood at the front of the church and promised to love one another for ever and ever. He waited while all

the ladies in hats dabbed
at their tears with their hankies and
hurried down the steps to the pavement. And he
waited while all the people who didn't want to walk
over the hill to the party took a seat in the minibus.

Then all the rest of them set off walking in a long
straggly line, down the lane, through the wood, and over
the hill towards Flora's field of buttercups. Jamie had
Angus in his backpack with his head sticking out so
Angus could see where they'd been, and when they
reached the top of the hill he turned round so Angus
could see where they were going.

"I certainly hope the wedding cake gets there safely,"
said Jamie's father.

"I hope the rain holds off," said Jamie's mother.

Then everyone straggled down the hill in a long line,
and into the field of buttercups.

It was a wonderful party. First Angus got covered in puffy yellow pollen from prancing through all the buttercups. Then, when Jamie had shaken that off, he got covered in petals from playing under the hawthorn hedges.

Jamie made a daisy-chain necklace for Flora, to go with her daisy hairslides.

Everyone loved the cake, which had reached the field safely (just as Flora had said it would).

And the rain held off (just as Flora had said it would).

Then Flora called everyone round her. "We're going to make our special fly-away balloon wishes now."

Out from behind the hedge came a floating mountain of shiny coloured balloons, all straining to escape up into the bright blue sky. Underneath was Mark, carefully holding the strings tight. He handed everyone a huge fat glossy balloon on a string. Daddy had a green one. Mummy's was purple. And the one he gave Jamie was buttercup yellow.

"Can Angus have one?" begged Jamie. "Can he have a red one, please? Red is his favourite colour. Angus really, really loves red balloons."

Mark looked down at Angus, tucked under Jamie's arm. "Did Angus get a proper invitation?" he asked. "Or did he just come along with you?"

"He had a proper invitation," Jamie told him. "Flora and I made it together when she came last time."

And the words "last time" made him feel sad, because now Flora was married maybe she wouldn't ever come to babysit for him again.

Mark saw his sad face and picked one of the red balloons out of his giant floating mountain.

"Angus can have his own balloon because there are exactly the same number of balloons as invitations.

And he can have a red one. I'll tie it safely round one of his legs." Mark tied a double bow, just to be sure.

"Now you hang on to Angus," he warned Jamie, "in case he floats up in the air with his balloon."

Jamie held Angus tighter. "Can you give me a double bow on my balloon as well?" he asked Mark.

"All right," said Mark, and tied the other balloon to Jamie's arm.

So now Jamie was standing in the circle with his own fat shiny yellow balloon floating up from one arm, and Angus tucked under the other arm with his fat shiny red balloon floating up from him.

Flora went round the circle with felt pens. "Make a wish," she told everyone. "Write it on the balloon."

Jamie asked Mummy, "Can I please wish to take my balloon home after the party?"

Mummy gave Jamie a little look. "Do you think the wish can come true," she asked, "if the balloon doesn't fly away?"

Jamie thought for a little. "Yes," he said firmly. "Yes. I think it can."

Mummy didn't argue. She went rushing off to hold Aunt Lilian's balloon while she wrote her wish on it.

"Maybe it can," agreed Daddy, hurrying off to hold Uncle Tony's balloon steady for him. "But I don't think you're supposed to be wishing for yourself."

Jamie looked round at all the people in the buttercup field, racking their brains to think of special wedding day wishes for Flora and Mark.

"Health!" Flora's mother was saying.

"Wealth!" said Aunt Lilian.

"Four bouncing babies!" suggested Uncle Tony.

"Perfect happiness!" said Mark's best friend.

"Long lives together!" said Flora's sister.

"A car that starts all through the winter!" said the vicar.

Jamie and Angus looked at one another. Jamie knew

what Angus was thinking. And Angus knew what Jamie was thinking.

When Mark came over to help Angus and Jamie write their wishes, Jamie said, "I wish that Angus doesn't have to let go of his beautiful fat red balloon, because he really, really, really loves balloons – especially red ones."

So Mark wrote that on Jamie's yellow balloon. Then he looked at Angus. "What about you?" he said. "What's your special fly-away wish for someone else?"

Angus looked shy.

"What Angus wishes," said Jamie, "is that, even though Flora is married to you now, she'll still sometimes come back to babysit for me."

"Really?" said Mark. "Is that so?" And in case Jamie's wish for Angus came true, and Angus didn't have to let his beautiful red balloon float away with all the others, Mark wrote Angus's wish for Jamie under Jamie's wish for Angus on the yellow one.

"Right," he said. "And now I'd better go and nibble the bride's ear, just like it says in the marriage rules."

Jamie watched him go back to Flora. After a moment he turned to Angus and told him, "It doesn't look to me as if Mark's nibbling. To me it looks more as if he's whispering."

But Angus was staring at buttercups and paying no attention.

"Time to let go of the balloons," said Flora a few minutes later. "Except for Angus's red one, which has to stay on earth for luck." She turned to Jamie. "If he doesn't mind."

"Oh, no," said Jamie. "He won't mind. He'll be quite pleased really."

"That's what I thought," said Flora. And she smiled.

Then everyone stood in a circle in the buttercups. Jamie's father untied the double bow on Jamie's arm, so the yellow balloon could go sailing up with the others. Jamie held the string tightly.

"One, two, three – go!" cried Flora, and everyone let go. Except for Angus's red one, all the balloons floated up, up, carrying their good wishes over the trees and up to the clouds – sky-high! And then everyone cheered and went on with the party.

Flora's been married for months now. But she still comes to babysit every now and again. Sometimes she brings Mark. Sometimes she doesn't. But she always brings a balloon because Angus really, really loves them – especially red ones.

And Jamie quite likes red ones too.

Tell Me the Story

"Tell me the story of how I grew

out of my buggy."

Daddy reeled around the bedroom, clutching his head. "Oh, no. Not again! I've told you a million, billion times."

"So, this time, tell Angus."

Daddy sank onto the end of the bed, while Jamie tucked Angus in neatly beside himself under the covers, with just his eyes and nose and front hooves sticking out.

"Quite sure he's comfy?" Daddy asked.

"Yes. Go on with the story."

Daddy turned to Angus. "Well, Angus. This is how it happened. Young Jamie here was getting on for nearly four whole years old—"

"I was three and a half," Jamie corrected him.

"Who's telling this story?" Daddy asked. "You, or me?"

"You," Jamie said.

"And who am I telling?"

"Angus."

"Right," Daddy said. "So don't interrupt."

And he went back to the tale of how Jamie grew out of his buggy.

"So, one day, as a treat for Granny's birthday, we all went on a visit to the Museum of Modern Art."

"You know Granny likes art," Jamie reminded Angus. "That's why she paints her own pictures and makes her own clay pots and bowls, and bends all sorts of odd bits of metal into fancy shapes to keep on her patio. And on Thursdays she even goes to college to teach other people how to do it."

"Wednesdays," said Jamie's father. "On Thursdays she takes you swimming."

"Who was telling that bit?" asked Jamie. "You, or me?"

"You were," said Daddy.

"And who was I telling?"

"Angus."

"That's right," said Jamie. And he waited for his father to get on with the story.

Daddy climbed into bed next to Angus, to be a little warmer and comfier, and carried on.

"So off we all went – Jamie and Granny and Mummy and me. And Jamie was sitting in his battered old buggy. And the museum is right at the top of the hill. So guess who had to push Jamie in his buggy all the way up to the top?"

There was a silence.

Jamie put his head down, close to Angus's snout.

"Angus guesses

60

that you did," he told his
father.

"And Angus is dead
right!" said Daddy. "I
had to push that great
big fat lazy tub of lard
called Jamie all the way
up the hill to the
museum."

"I wasn't a great
big fat lazy tub
of lard," Jamie

assured Angus. "I was perfectly normal. It's just that my
legs were tired."

"Your legs weren't tired," said Daddy. "You just liked
being pushed. You just liked sitting there, all comfy in
your battered and rusty old buggy, with your thumb in
your mouth, watching the world go by."

Jamie sat quietly for a while, remembering sitting all
comfy in his battered and rusty old buggy, with his
thumb in his mouth, watching the world go by.

"*I* was the one with tired legs," Daddy grumbled to Angus. "And tired arms. And tired back. And tired every bit of me."

"Go on with the story," said Jamie.

Daddy got on with the story. "So then we trailed Granny all the way round the great big Museum of Modern Art," he explained to Angus. "First we went through the rooms with all the big splotches. Then we went through the rooms with all the claggy lumps. And then we went outside in the gardens to look at all the clumps of tangled metal."

"Don't listen to him," Jamie said to Angus. "He says it that way to tease Granny. But Granny says what he *means* is that we went through the rooms with all the lovely modern paintings, and then through the rooms with all the interesting pottery, and then out in the gardens to look at all the amazing metal sculptures."

"And I know you'll find this hard to believe, Angus," Daddy said. "But, the whole time, this great big fat lazy tub of lard sitting here in the bed beside you wouldn't

63

get out of his buggy, even though he was getting on for nearly four whole years old."

"Three and a half," corrected Jamie. "And Daddy's just being rude. He does it to tease me."

Daddy turned to Angus. "And then we went home. And, even then, this great big fat lazy lump wouldn't get out of his buggy and walk for a little bit. Even though it was downhill all the way."

"I was tired," said Jamie.

"You were idle," said Daddy.

Angus gazed ahead sadly.

"Yes," Daddy said. "It's a shocking story, Angus, isn't it? And it gets *worse.*"

Angus's eyes were very wide.

"Only because Daddy got cross and lost his temper," Jamie explained to Angus.

"Who's telling this bit of the story?" asked Daddy.

"You are," said Jamie.

"So I got cross," said Daddy. "I'd pushed this great fat idle tub of lard all the way up the hill. And I'd pushed him all the way round the museum and the gardens.

And now I was having to push him all the way back down the hill again."

"Pull me, he means," explained Jamie. "To stop the buggy running away with me down the hill."

"And by the time we got to Granny's house, my arms were aching even worse than my legs and my back," Daddy explained to Angus. "And still Jamie wouldn't get out and walk. So when we reached our own gate, I said to him, 'You can at least get out now and walk up your own garden path.'"

He leaned down to Angus. "And do you know what this precious Jamie of yours said?"

Angus waited on tenterhooks.

"He said, 'No!' Can you believe that, Angus? Getting on for nearly four whole years old—"

"Three and a half," corrected Jamie.

"And he just said, 'No!' Good thing you weren't there, Angus. You'd have been shocked. Someone of that age, refusing to get out of their battered and rusty old buggy and walk up their own garden path."

Angus looked shocked.

"So I did what anybody would have done, Angus. I lost my temper. I tipped this great big fat idle tub of lard out onto the grass, and I stamped on that rusty and battered old buggy over and over till it was just a heap of tangled metal, and nobody was ever going to be able to sit in it ever again."

"There," Jamie said proudly. "That is the story of how I grew out of my buggy."

Daddy got out from under the covers and kissed Jamie, shook hand and hoof with Angus, and switched off the bedside lamp.

"Aren't you going to tell Angus the very end of the story before you go downstairs to Mummy?" Jamie asked.

Daddy hurried to the door. "No."

"I'll tell him, then," warned Jamie. "After you've gone."

Daddy shook a finger. "Don't you listen to him, Angus. He'll only be saying it to tease me."

And off he went downstairs to Mummy.

In the dark, Jamie told Angus the very end of the story. How Granny had come round the next morning and seen the tangly mess of battered, rusty, stamped-on

buggy and said to Daddy, "Oh, look! I knew you only said you didn't like modern art to tease me! Now I see you've even made a lovely bit of it all on your own in your very own garden."

And she'd taken it home before the dustbin men got it, and she kept it on her patio to tease him back.

Temper, Temper!
by Jamie's father
(Rusty metal and webbing)

Strawberry
Creams

Jamie had stomach-ache.

"Where, exactly?" Mummy asked, giving him a little prod.

"Ouch!" Jamie told her.

Next day it was no better, so they went down to the clinic, where Nurse asked Jamie if she could take a look.

"Where, exactly?" she asked him, pressing his stomach.

"Ouch!" Jamie told her.

Nurse sent him in to Dr Helen.

"Where, exactly?" she asked, leaning over to press gently all round his belly-button.

"Ouch!" Jamie told her. "Ouch, ouch, *ouch*!" (He was getting fed up with all this prodding and pressing.)

In the end Dr Helen told Mummy, "I think we're going to have to bring him in."

Where, exactly? thought Jamie. He looked anxiously at Angus and Angus looked anxiously back at him. "Can Angus come with me?" he asked.

"Of course," said Dr Helen. "So long as he knows how to keep his horns to himself in bed, and to keep quiet when other people are sleeping."

So Jamie and Angus went into hospital. Jamie had brand-new pyjamas with giant froggy pockets, and Angus wore a ribbon round his neck with a label giving Jamie's name and ward number (which was 17). They had a bed by the window. In the next bed was Mahailia, who had long black hair, pink pyjamas, a huge box of chocolates and an enormous fat stuffed seal called Nafisa.

"What's wrong with you, then?" Jamie's mother asked.

In answer, Mahailia lifted up her pyjama top to show them a neat line of tiny stitches right across her tummy.

"This," she said. "But I'm much better now." And as soon as her mother and father had gone back home to look after her sister, she wandered off to watch television in a little room with glass walls at the end of the ward.

Jamie played cards with Mummy. And then he let Daddy read him a story. And then he said to his parents, "You can go home now, too, if you like."

"That's all right," Daddy said. "We're happy to stay with you."

"Oh," Jamie said.

So he played cards with Daddy. And then he let Mummy read him a story. And then he tried again. "You can go home now, if you like."

"Certainly not," Daddy said.

But Mummy was looking at Jamie, and suddenly she grinned and said, "Would you and Angus like Daddy and me to go home, so you can watch telly with Mahailia?"

"Yes, please," said Jamie. "But don't forget to come back in the morning."

So Mummy and Daddy went off, and Jamie wandered down the ward to the room at the end with the glass walls. He stood in the doorway for a while, watching the telly. Then he changed his mind and went back to his own bed to play cards with Angus and read him a story.

Then Mahailia came back and sat on his bed, and they played cards in two teams: Angus and Jamie versus Nafisa and Mahailia.

"I'd give you one of my chocolates," Mahailia told Jamie afterwards. "But I'm keeping the last ones specially for the day when they tell me that I can go home again."

Then she got back in her own bed and went to sleep.

Jamie and Angus played cards a little longer, and Jamie couldn't help noticing that Angus kept looking at the big box of chocolates on top of Mahailia's bedside cabinet.

Perhaps he was curious about how many she was keeping specially for the day when they told her that she could go home again. After all, it was a big box. Jamie thought Mahailia wouldn't mind if Angus was allowed to lift the lid a tiny bit with his nose – just to take a quick peek.

Jamie held Angus up, and Angus lifted the edge of the lid with his nose. Inside was a sea of empty brown wrappers, but only three chocolates left.

Only three.

Three…

Three she was keeping specially.

Jamie thought Angus might want to know what sort they were, in case they were the kind that he didn't like anyway. But they were all strawberry creams, and Angus really did like strawberry creams. (So did Jamie.)

Angus didn't mean to help Jamie choose one.

And he certainly didn't mean to help Jamie take it.

Or eat it.

It was just that Angus and Jamie weren't used to being in hospital. And Jamie wasn't used to being in a strange bed. And he certainly wasn't used to having someone else's box of chocolates so close that the last three could practically jump into his mouth. All three!

Three she was keeping specially.

Next morning Jamie woke up feeling terrible. Terrible!
And it wasn't just the stomach-ache. He peeped round
to see if Mahailia was already pointing her finger at
him, ready to say, "You stole my last three chocolates!"

But she wasn't there!

One of the nurses saw him staring at the empty bed.
"Don't look so worried," she told him. "Mahailia's just
gone to have her stitches out because she's going home
today."

Going home? Jamie looked guiltily at Angus, and

Angus looked guiltily back at him. They were in trouble now. As soon as Mahailia came back, she'd look in her chocolate box and find it empty.

Jamie was still sitting worrying when his mother came. She gave him a hug and said, "My word, you look miserable!"

He couldn't help it – he burst into tears.

Mummy hugged him tighter. "Shall I read you a story?"

Jamie shook his head.

"Shall I play cards with you?"

Jamie shook his head again.

"Well, shall I go off and find the lady with the little shop on wheels, and buy you a brand-new fancy colouring book and a nice pack of felt pens?"

And because he was fed up with shaking his head, Jamie found himself nodding.

While his mother was gone, Dr Helen arrived with a crowd of young doctors in white coats carrying clipboards and pens.

"Good morning, Jamie," she said to him. "Today I've

brought a whole gang to look at your very interesting tummy."

There they all were: short doctors, tall doctors, pink doctors, brown doctors, lady doctors, men doctors, cheerful doctors, worried doctors. They stood in a circle round his bed, looking at Jamie until he felt even *worse*.

"May I?" asked Dr Helen, and she reached down to lift his pyjama top with the giant froggy pockets.

Not so politely, Jamie tugged it down again.

"I expect you're fed up with everyone wanting to prod your stomach," said Dr Helen. "But it's a shame, because all these young doctors here could learn quite a lot from just one little press."

Jamie just scowled and tugged his pyjama top down even further.

"Please?" Dr Helen asked. "We're only here to help."

But Jamie wasn't in the mood for "please". He was about as fed up as a body can be. He was sick of having stomach-ache. He was cross with himself for eating Mahailia's last three strawberry creams, and he was worried that, when she found out, she'd think he and

Angus were mean and horrible, and not to be trusted. And he was sick of everyone standing around wanting to lift his pyjama top to press him and prod him.

Suddenly Jamie had an idea to make them all go away at once.

He raised his pyjama top. "All right," he told them. "But you'll have to pay. And it's expensive. It's a penny a press and two pennies a prod."

And he waited for them to move on to another bed, to someone who wasn't so rude and ungrateful.

Dr Helen waggled a finger. "It was free yesterday," she reminded him.

"That was a special offer," Jamie told her firmly. "And it's over now."

He sat in his bed with his arms folded, waiting for them to move off. But no one did. First they all looked at one another. Then one or two of them started grinning. And the young man who was nearest rooted deep in the pockets of his white coat, searching for coins.

Finding a penny, he held it out. "I'll have a little press, please."

What could poor Jamie do now? He wasn't allowed
to take money from strangers! He shook his head. But
instead of dropping the coin back in his pocket, the
doctor laid it on the bedside cabinet, right between
Angus's front hooves.

Jamie gave up. He'd made a bargain so he had to
keep it. Sighing, he lifted his pyjama top and waited to
be peered at and pressed and prodded.

The young man leaned over and gave Jamie's stomach
a very gentle little press. "Mmmmm!" he said. "Now
that *is* interesting."

Another doctor fished deep in her pocket and put two
pennies down in front of Angus. "If it's that interesting,
I'll have a prod, please."

Jamie felt guilty, seeing the pennies between Angus's
hooves. So he said, "You can have a free press too."

"Bargain!" said the doctor. And, once she'd finished, she told everyone, "That was worth every penny, if you want my opinion."

So then all of them wanted a go at pressing and prodding. The pile of pennies between Angus's hooves grew higher and higher. Some had to borrow from their mates. Some came back for seconds. And one of them even fetched out her chequebook.

"I'm afraid Angus doesn't accept cheques," said Jamie. "Or Visa. Or Switch."

So that doctor had to go free. By the end, every last one of them had had a turn; and all agreed that Jamie's was, without a doubt, the most interesting stomach any of them had ever paid to press.

And then they all moved off down the ward to look at someone else. Jamie slid out of bed and scooped the money into his giant froggy pockets just as his mother and the lady with the shop on wheels came through the swing doors.

While his mother was busy talking to Dr Helen, Jamie asked the lady,

"Please, do you have
any strawberry creams?"

She rooted through her packets. "Lemon ... and coffee ... and – yes! – you're lucky. Here's a packet of strawberry creams."

"How many are there?" asked Jamie.

She counted through the cellophane. "Five."

"Goody!" said Jamie. He scooped all the money out of his pyjama pockets into her hands, and together they counted it.

"Just enough!" she said.

Quickly he took the packet. While Angus watched him anxiously, Jamie lifted the lid of Mahailia's box and tipped in three chocolates. Then he put the lid back on safely and climbed into bed again. He was still sitting, good as gold, playing cards with his mother, when Mahailia came back to show him the marks where they'd taken out her stitches.

Jamie stayed in hospital for six whole days. He finished the colouring book and used up the felt pens. Everyone visited – Granny and Flora and even Uncle Edward – and everyone kept asking why, even after the doctors had fixed his stomach-ache, he still wouldn't eat the two strawberry creams on top of his cabinet.

"Angus and I are saving them specially," he kept having to explain to them, "for the day that they tell us that we can go home again."

The Perfect Day

Jamie leaned over the arm of the sofa
and dipped his finger into Daddy's drink.
Then he sucked it and made his
that-tastes-horrible face.

"Is it *true*," he asked, "that grown-ups like drinking that stuff more than they like drinking Hairy Joe's Jungle Juice?"

"Yes, I'm afraid a good number of us do," admitted Daddy.

Jamie took an olive out of the dish on the arm of the

sofa and nibbled the end till his mouth went all puckery.

"And is it *true* that grown-ups like this nasty sour green taste more than they like Mr Munchie Monster Mashdrops?"

"Yup," said his father. "And if you're not planning on finishing that olive, you can give it to me rather than waste it."

He opened his mouth wide and Jamie popped the olive in. Then Jamie and Angus lay on their backs on the sofa beside Daddy, with their legs pointing up to the ceiling.

"And is it *true*," Jamie asked, "that grown-ups prefer sitting the right way up in chairs?"

"Indeed they do," said Daddy. "Except, perhaps, for your Uncle Edward." He glanced at the clock on the mantelpiece. "Isn't it getting on for your bedtime?"

"No," Jamie said, and drifted through to the other room, where Mummy was busy with her papers.

He rested his elbows on the desk and watched for a bit.

"Sleepy?" Mummy asked him.

"No."

"It's almost your bedtime."

"No, it isn't," said Jamie. Then he asked, "Is it *true* that grown-ups are happy to go upstairs to bed almost as soon as it's time?"

Mummy looked at Jamie over her spectacles. "Jamie," she told him, "I'd go back to bed practically straight after breakfast if I could. And sleep for a whole week."

"A whole *week*?"

"Absolutely."

Jamie stared for a while in amazement. Then, in case the word "sleep" had reminded her, he went back to Daddy, who was watching the news, which was people droning on about banks, shares and money.

"Is it *true*," Jamie asked him, "that grown-ups like watching the news more than they like watching Piggily-Pig cartoons?"

"Well, I do," sighed Daddy. "Whenever I get the opportunity to do so without interruption." He glanced at the clock again. "Are you *sure* it's not your bedtime?"

Jamie hurried back to the other room. "And is it *true*," he asked, "that grown-ups prefer to stay on the path in the park, and not walk with their arms out along the tops of walls, and not stamp in puddles in their wellies, or make ice squeak with their shoes?"

"All true," said Mummy. "Unless you're counting Uncle Edward as a grown-up, which personally I wouldn't."

Jamie went back to Daddy. "And is it *true*," he asked, "that grown-ups don't really care much for being held upside down, or swung round really fast?"

"Gospel truth," said his father. "And a goodly number of us could live quite happily without swings, merry-go-rounds, ghost trains or flumes in the swimming pool."

"Not without *flumes*?" said Jamie.

"Yes," his father assured him. "Some of us could most particularly do without flumes."

He looked at the clock again.

"*And* without people who are still hanging around ten minutes after their bedtime."

So Jamie went off to bed. On the way up the stairs he said to Angus, "Tomorrow, for one day only, as an experiment, I'm going to give myself a grown-up's perfect day."

Angus just stared.

In the morning when Daddy came in to wake him, Jamie buried his head in the pillow just like Mummy and said, "I'm *shattered*. I could sleep for a *week*."

"What was that?" said his father. "I can't hear you. You're all muffled."

Jamie lifted his head from the pillow and said it more clearly. "I could sleep for a week."

"Tough," said his father. "Now hop out of bed and put on these clothes. Pronto."

Jamie looked at the cheerful blue trousers his father was laying out for him – not exactly a grown-up's perfect colour.

"Have I got anything a bit more *grey*?"

His father peered in the cupboard. "We have purple. And dark red. Bottle green. And stripy."

"Oh, well," said Jamie. And he chose the bottle green, because that was a colour he'd seen on Uncle Edward.

While he was dressing, Jamie explained to Angus, "I shan't be talking to you quite so much today. Grown-ups don't do that. I know Daddy sometimes says 'Good morning, Angus' as he walks past you. And Mummy often says things like 'Oh, Angus, how come you fetched up *there*?' or 'How on earth did you get so grubby?' But they don't really *talk* to you – not like I do. And so I'm afraid, for you, today's going to be pretty quiet."

And Angus understood, though you could tell from the look on his face that he didn't really like it and he wasn't really happy.

At breakfast Angus watched as Jamie ate his boiled egg and then turned the shell over carefully in the eggcup and reached for a felt pen to draw some straggly hair and a crosspatch face.

Then Angus watched as Jamie put the felt pen down again.

"Grown-ups don't draw on their eggs," explained Jamie, before remembering he wasn't really talking to Angus today. He could tell Angus thought it was a waste of a good shell, but he didn't say more. He just slid off his chair to get all his things ready.

On the way through the park, Jamie kept to the path. He walked round the puddles and didn't balance on the tops of walls, and they arrived even before Mrs Hardy had opened the big doors.

Perhaps that's why grown-ups do it that way, thought Jamie (though he personally didn't think arriving early was worth it).

Since Angus wasn't there to watch, he took a break from having a grown-up's perfect day till it was time to go.

Granny had come to pick him up to take him swimming. As they walked out, he asked her, "What would I be talking to you about now if I were a grown-up?"

"The weather?" suggested Granny. "Just perhaps for a moment, until we got started."

"All right," said Jamie. He had a think and then said conversationally, "I reckon it's getting a little bit black over Bill's mother's."

Granny stared.

"I got that from Lucy," said Jamie. "She learned it from Arif. He says it means it's going to rain."

"Honestly!" said Granny. "The things you lot pick up!"

And since she suddenly sounded grown up enough for two, Jamie reckoned he could take a break and talk about Piggily-Pig.

At the pool Granny asked, "Which flume for starters?"

"Neither," said Jamie. "Flumes don't appeal today."

"Really?"

"Yes, really."

"Fancy!" said Granny, and joined the queue for the curly one.

When they got home, Mummy said, "Tonight, for supper, there's a choice. Spaghetti hoops, or what we're having, which has olives in it."

Jamie sighed. Angus was looking at him most forlornly. He'd had a boring time alone at home, and now, instead of being cuddled and talked to and offered his very own spaghetti hoop to balance on his nose, he was going to have to carry on standing by the plate rack, all alone, watching Jamie struggle through some fancy supper with olives.

But this was an experiment. It was supposed to be a grown-up's perfect day.

"I'll have what you're having," Jamie said sadly. "But only a little. Not that much."

Even though Daddy kept trading lumps of buttered bread for Jamie's piles of olive bits, Jamie was still hungry after supper. Mummy said he could have something from the jar. He dipped his hand in. There were Spinny Wheels and Coconut Glories and Peppermint Hoolas.

Then he remembered.

He took his hand out. "I'll just have a nice fresh orange," he said wistfully.

After supper Jamie was sent for his bath. Grown-ups don't play in baths, so he left Angus standing by the plate rack, looking lonely, and went upstairs with heavy heart.

"Bubbles?" Daddy offered.

Did grown-ups have bubbles? Sometimes they did.

But what was the point of bubbles

if Angus wasn't there to admire Bubble Mountain's giant bubbly peaks, and Bubble Monster's fat white bubbling hands, and Jamie's special Bubble Soup, and the little lakes in Bubble Land?

"No thanks," said Jamie. "I don't think I'll bother."

Jamie sat in his bath. He was bored. He was hungry. He was lonely. And he had things he wanted to tell Angus.

And then he realized. This was a grown-up's perfect day. So he could choose his own bedtime.

Jamie let out the water and wrapped himself up in his towel and went downstairs.

"I'm turning in now," he told Mummy, just like Daddy did.

Mummy glanced at the clock. "Really?"

"Yes," Jamie said. "It's been a long and tiring day." (That was what she often said.)

"And now I
think I'll hit the road
and have an early night."
(That was his granny.)

"I want to be really
on top in the morning."
(That was Flora, when she
didn't want his parents
to stay out late.)

He tried to think of something Uncle Edward might ever have said about going to bed early. But nothing came to mind.

"Right," he said, picking up Angus. "I'll just put this away tidily in my bedroom."

He could tell Angus didn't care much for being called "this". Or for being tidied.

But things were desperate.

Jamie put Angus tidily away in his shoebox shed and got into bed. Mummy brought him some cocoa to make up for the olives, and read him a story. Then she turned out the light and left the door open.

Jamie told the air around him (but mostly Angus), "That is the last grown-up's perfect day I'm ever having till I'm grown up properly. Tomorrow I'm going straight back to living my own way."

He wasn't sure, but through the darkness he thought he heard the noise a little Highland bull would make if it were sighing with relief.

"Tomorrow," Jamie told the air around him (but mostly Angus), "we will have our own perfect day, I promise."

And, next day,
that is exactly what they
had. Angus and Jamie.
Jamie and Angus.

Anne Fine was elected to take on the prestigious position of Children's Laureate in 2001. A highly acclaimed author, she has won the Smarties Book Prize, the Guardian Children's Fiction Award and twice won both the Carnegie Medal and the Whitbread Children's Book Award, most recently for *The Tulip Touch*. She was also voted Children's Author of the Year in 1990 and 1993. Her book *Goggle-eyes* was dramatized as a BBC TV serial and *Madame Doubtfire* was turned into the hugely successful Hollywood film, *Mrs Doubtfire*. She has two daughters and lives in County Durham.

You can find out more about Anne Fine and her books by visiting her website at www.annefine.co.uk

Penny Dale is one of this country's leading illustrators of children's books. For Walker she has illustrated the picture books *The Stopwatch*; *Once There Were Giants*; *Rosie's Babies* (shortlisted for the Kate Greenaway Medal and Winner of the Best Books for Babies Award); and *Cuddly Bear*; as well as her own stories *Bet You Can't!*; *Ten in the Bed*; *Ten Out of Bed*; *The Elephant Tree*; *All About Alice*; *Daisy Rabbit's Tree House*; *Wake Up, Mr B!* (shortlisted for the Kate Greenaway Medal); and *Big Brother, Little Brother*. Penny is married with one daughter and lives in South Wales.